To my parents, I love you more than you could ever know.

With all of my love and my deepest respect and gratitude,

Sherri

www.mascotbooks.com

For more information, please contact:
Mascot Books
560 Herndon Parkway #120
Herndon, VA 20170
info@mascotbooks.com

CPSIA Code: PRT0213A
ISBN-10: 1620860880
ISBN-13: 9781620860885

Printed in the United States

There is 1 University of Alabama and we're number 1. When it comes to being champions, we get it done.

There are 2 sides to the coin the ref tosses in the air. The winning team chooses defense or offense – that's fair.

ALABAMA 3 QUARTER 1 VISITOR 0

We score 3 points when a field goal
is kicked. When we do it right,
our rivals are licked!

Each game has 4 quarters, sixty minutes in all. That's an awfully long time to play with a ball.

4

Count the 5 cheerleaders
stirring up the crowd.
Once they get started,
it's really loud!

A touchdown gives us 6 points.

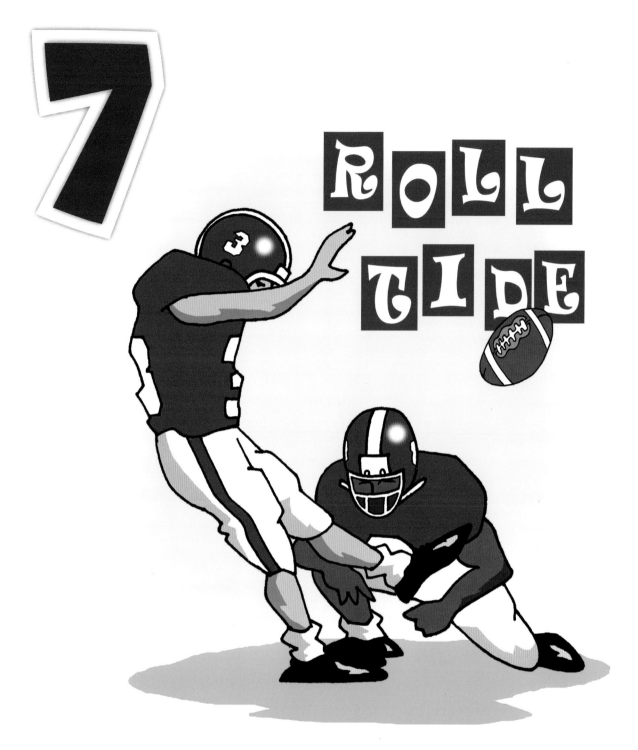

**With a good kick we get 7.
Our fans scream so loud
you could hear them in the heavens!**

Count the 8 fans with posters saying "ROLL TIDE!" They cheer it at each game with gusto and pride!

Count 9 fans
wearing crimson and white caps.
After the game,
it's time for a nap.

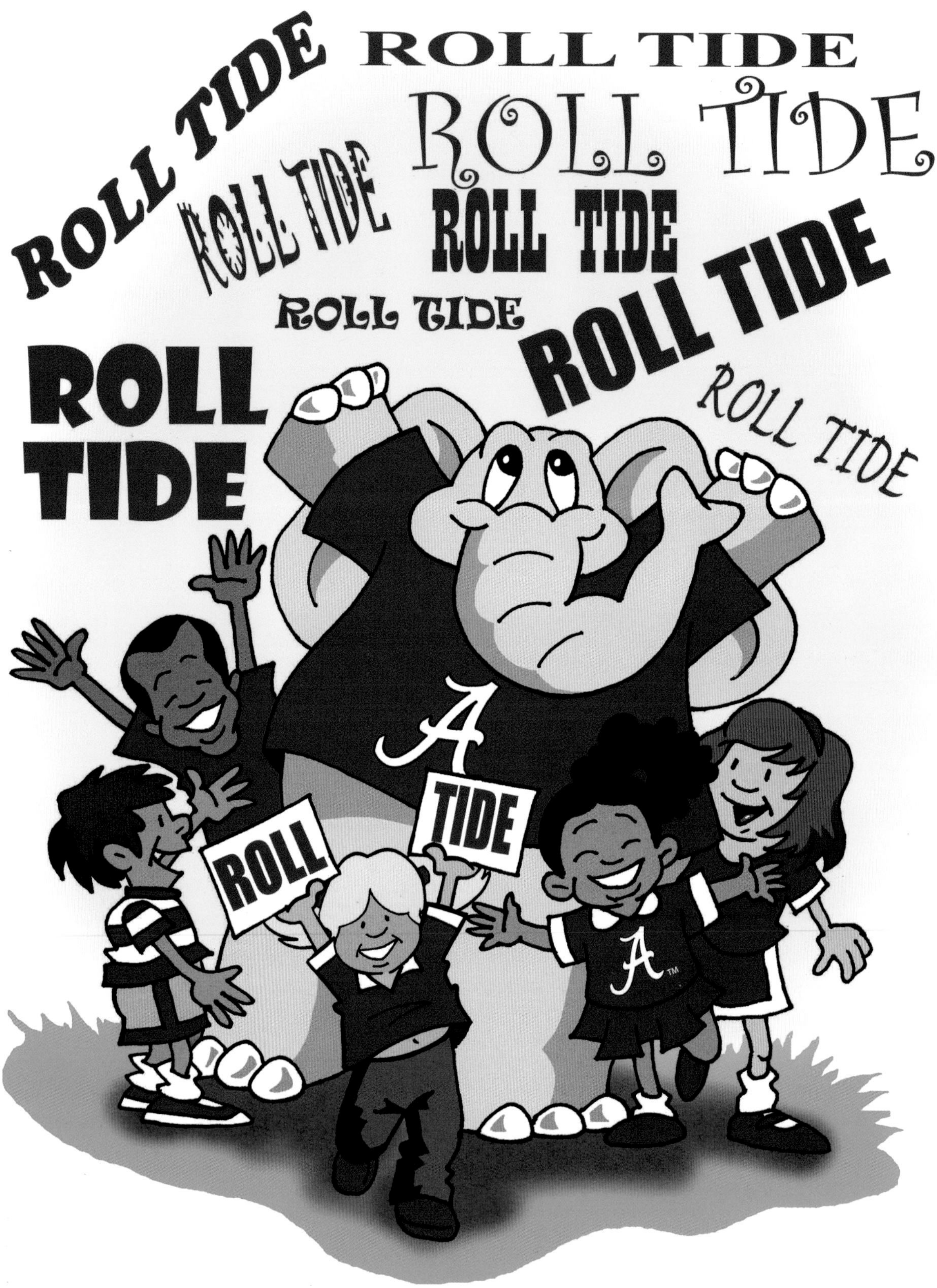
ROLL TIDE
ROLL TIDE
ROLL TIDE
ROLL TIDE
ROLL TIDE
ROLL TIDE
ROLL TIDE
ROLL TIDE
ROLL TIDE
ROLL
TIDE

Hey Alabama fans—
cheer with Big Al 10 times!
All together now,
let's cheer one big "ROLL TIDE!"

About the Author

Sherri Graves Smith, a graduate of the University of Alabama, is a lifelong avid reader. At an early age, Sherri's parents instilled in her a great love of reading books which she still enjoys doing every day. Her parents were also instrumental in grooming her into a huge fan of Alabama football. To date, Sherri and her family "dress out" for Alabama football games and cheer on the Crimson Tide each fall.

Sherri volunteered to tutor and read to children because of the positive difference reading has made in her life. This led her to start writing children's books. In writing *Counting With Big Al*, Sherri wanted to make reading fun, bring in some Alabama tradition, and share in the joy and the experience of passing on the love of books to another generation. She hopes that you enjoyed reading her book as much as she enjoyed writing it!

ROLL TIDE ROLL!

Have a book idea?

Contact us at:

Mascot Books

560 Herndon Parkway

Suite 120

Herndon, VA

info@mascotbooks.com | www.mascotbooks.com

Bonus Coloring Book!

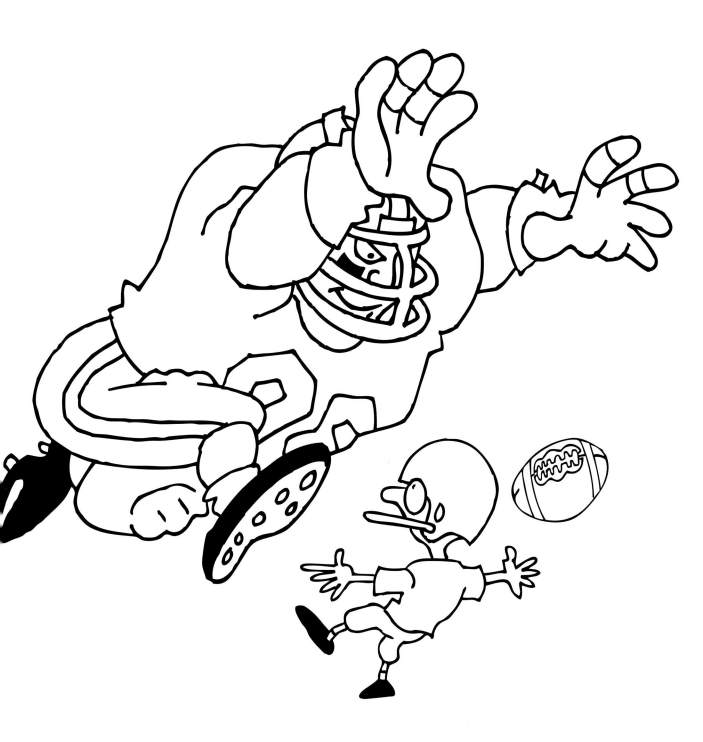

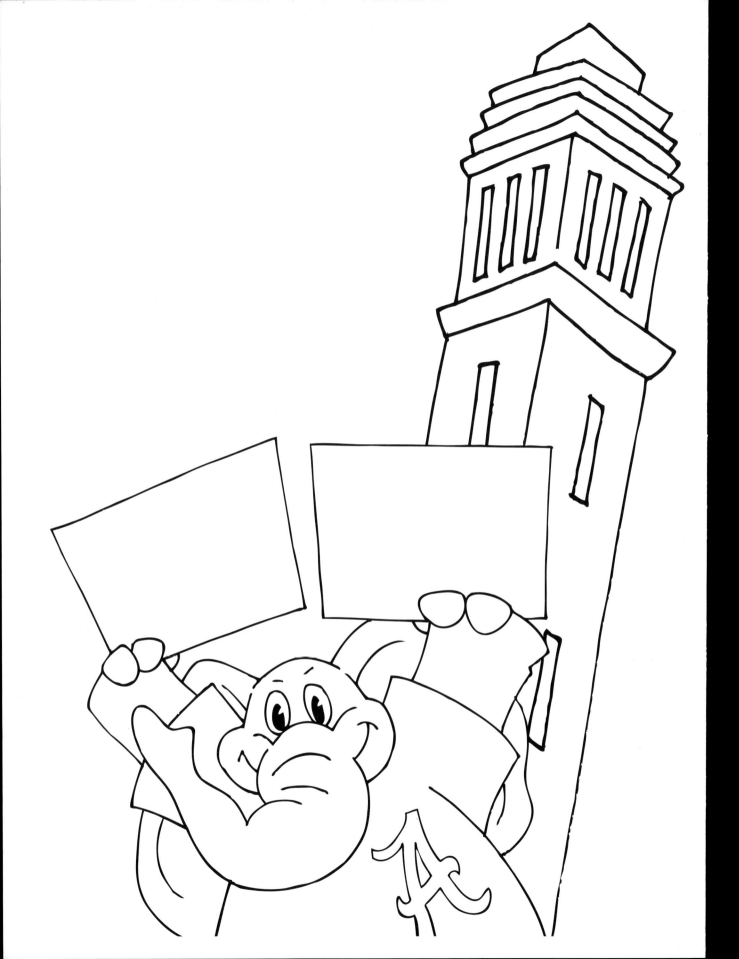